Any inquiries in regards to this book should be addressed to:
Forever Young Publishers
P.O. Box 216; Niles, Michigan 49120

Visit us on the Web:
www.foreveryoungpublishers.com
e-mail: cheri@foreveryoungpublishers.com

First Edition
Printed and bound in Canada
Friesens of Altona, Manitoba

Publisher's Cataloging-in-Publication
(Provided by Quality Books, Inc.)

Hallwood, Cheri L.
The curious polka-dot present / written by Cheri L.
Hallwood ; illustrated by Patricia M. Rose.
p. cm.
SUMMARY: A little girl waits anxiously for a surprise
package to come by mail. When the mysterious gift
arrives for her birthday she can't imagine who sent the
colorful present. She and her mother open it to find
something handmade with love from her grandma.
Audience: Ages 2-8.
LCCN 2006910827
ISBN-13: 978-0-9774422-1-8
ISBN-10: 0-9774422-1-7

1. Birthdays--Juvenile fiction. 2. Gifts--Juvenile
fiction. 3. Grandparent and child--Juvenile fiction.
[1. Birthdays--Fiction. 2. Gifts--Fiction. 3. Grandmothers--
Fiction. 4. Stories in rhyme.] I. Rose, Patricia M., ill. II. Title.

PZ8.3.H1597Cur 2007   [E]
QBI07-600060

Author's dedication
to . . .

. . . my Grandma Adeline, for loving memories.
. . . my mom, Bettie, and mother-in-law, Maisie,
for having been the very best Grandmas.
. . . my granddaughters, Ali, Aubrey, Hannah, Maisie Kate,
and my granddaughters who are on their way.
What joy you bring to my life.

Illustrator's dedication
to . . .

. . . the loving memory of my dad, Ted, who is greatly missed.
. . . the promise of the future with the anticipated
arrival of our first grandchild.

Special thanks
to . . .

. . . my family and friends for always being there.
. . . Patricia M. Rose for her talent and friendship.
. . . Joya Helmuth for her special contribution to this book.
. . . Shannon Brewer for her love of words
and as editor of this book.

May all your days
be Special!
Cheri L. Hallwood

A book from
Forever Young Publishers
for

The Curious Polka~Dot Present

Written by
Cheri L. Hallwood

Illustrated by
Patricia M. Rose

How impatiently I have watched
From the window in my room,

Waiting for something special

Mommy said is coming very soon.

It should be here any day.

Something Special,

sent with love,

From someone far away.

Then... early this morning,

At exactly
"eight-thirty-eight,"

I awoke to see a
curious
present

Sitting by the
front yard gate.

It was large and oddly shaped

wrapped in polka~dots and stripes,

tied up in an orange ribbon

with a card tucked just inside.

"It's here! It's here!" I shouted,

as I raced for the door.

Could this be the

"Something Special"

I had been waiting for?

Down the path to the gate I ran

lickety~split all the way.

'cause I knew, without a doubt,

Today's my very

"Special Day!"

As each step took me closer

I soon began

to hear,

My own little heartbeat
pitter~patter in my ear.

What could it be?

I did not have ONE clue!

Who did it come from?

What should I do?

So I gently gathered it up with my arms all around,

Trying hard not to tear it,

Or drop it on the ground.

Then off to my room

with the present I went,

Still wondering what was inside

And from whom it was sent.

My! This polka-dot present,

Although oddly shaped,

Seemed quite light to the touch

And was very well taped.

Quickly

but

carefully,

As Mommy opened the card

That had

been tucked

just inside.

Happy Birthday

"HAPPY BIRTHDAY"
it read

In bright letters

of red, green, and blue.

I hope you enjoy what

Grandma has made

"With Love"

especially for you!